AnnA HiBiSCUS
AND HER
AMAZING
FAMILY

Other books by Atinuke

Too Small Tola
Too Small Tola and the Three Fine Girls
Too Small Tola Gets Tough
Too Small Tola Makes It Count

Anna Hibiscus
Hooray for Anna Hibiscus!
Good Luck, Anna Hibiscus!
Have Fun, Anna Hibiscus!
Welcome Home, Anna Hibiscus!
Go Well, Anna Hibiscus!
Love from Anna Hibiscus!
You're Amazing, Anna Hibiscus!

The No. 1 Car Spotter
The No. 1 Car Spotter and the Firebird
The No. 1 Car Spotter and the Car Thieves
The No. 1 Car Spotter Goes to School
The No. 1 Car Spotter and the Broken Road
The No. 1 Car Spotter Fights the Factory

For younger readers

Anna Hibiscus' Song
Splash, Anna Hibiscus!
Double Trouble for Anna Hibiscus!
Baby Goes to Market
B Is for Baby
Baby, Sleepy Baby
Catch That Chicken!
Hugo

Non-fiction

Africa, Amazing Africa: Country by Country

ANNA HIBISCUS

AND HER AMAZING FAMILY

Atinuke

illustrated by
Lauren Tobia

This is a work of fiction. Names, characters, places and incidents are either the product of the author's imagination or, if real, used fictitiously. All statements, activities, stunts, descriptions, information and material of any other kind contained herein are included for entertainment purposes only and should not be relied on for accuracy or replicated as they may result in injury.

First published individually as *Anna Hibiscus* (2007) and *Hooray for Anna Hibiscus!* (2008) by Walker Books Ltd
87 Vauxhall Walk, London SE11 5HJ

This edition published 2025

2 4 6 8 10 9 7 5 3 1

Text © 2007, 2008 Atinuke
Illustrations © 2007, 2008 Lauren Tobia

The right of Atinuke and Lauren Tobia to be identified as author and illustrator respectively of this work has been asserted in accordance with the Copyright, Designs and Patents Act 1988

EU Authorized Representative: HackettFlynn Ltd, 36 Cloch Choirneal, Balrothery, Co. Dublin, K32 C942, Ireland. EU@walkerpublishinggroup.com

This book has been typeset in Stempel Schneidler

Printed and bound by CPI Group (UK) Ltd, Croydon CR0 4YY

All rights reserved. No part of this book may be reproduced, transmitted or stored in an information retrieval system in any form or by any means, graphic, electronic or mechanical, including photocopying, taping and recording, without prior written permission from the publisher. Additionally, no part of this book may be used or reproduced in any manner for the purpose of training artificial intelligence technologies or systems, nor for text and data mining.

British Library Cataloguing in Publication Data:
a catalogue record for this book is available from the British Library

ISBN 978-1-5295-2689-9

www.walker.co.uk

Contents

Anna Hibiscus 6
   Anna Hibiscus on Holiday 9
   Auntie Comfort 37
   Anna Hibiscus Sells Oranges 67
   Sweet Snow 85

Hooray for Anna Hibiscus! 114
   Anna 'biscus! Sing! 117
   Your Hair, Anna Hibiscus! 145
   Anna Hibiscus
      and the New Generator 173
   The Other Side of the City 199

ANNA HIBISCUS

by Atinuke
illustrated by Lauren Tobia

WALKER
BOOKS

For the children of Fachongle
A.

For Paul, Lizzie and Alice,
my family and friends
L.T.

Anna Hibiscus on Holiday

Anna Hibiscus lives in Africa. Amazing
Africa. In a country called Nigeria. Na-wa-oh
Nigeria! Na-wa-oh is for something
surprising. And Nigeria is surprising! Anna
Hibiscus lives in an old white house. A
wonderful house inside a big compound.
The trees are full of juicy fruit and the
flowers are full of sweet nectar because
this is Nigeria, and Nigeria can be like this.
Outside the compound is the city of Lagos.

An amazing city of lagoons and bridges and roads, of skyscrapers and shanty towns.

Anna Hibiscus lives with her mother, who is from Canada; her father, who is from Nigeria; her grandmother and her grandfather; her aunties and her uncles; lots and lots of cousins; and her twin baby brothers, Double and Trouble.

There are so many people in Anna's family that even she cannot count them all.

Anna Hibiscus is never lonely. There are always cousins to play and fight with; uncles and aunties are always laughing and shouting; and her mother or father and grandmother or grandfather are always around.

To be alone in Anna Hibiscus's house you have to hide. Sometimes Anna squeezes into some cool, dusty, forgotten place and waits for that exciting moment when her family begins to call – and then a cousin or uncle finds her and her aunties thank God!

One day, Anna's mother told the family that in Canada she grew up in a house with only her mother and her father.

"What!" cried Auntie Grace. "All alone? Only the three of you?"

"Yes, and I had a room all of my own," Anna's mother said wistfully.

Anna's grandmother looked at her. "You had to sleep alone?" she asked.

"It was not a punishment," Anna's mother said. "It was a good thing to have my own room."

Anna Hibiscus and her cousins looked at each other. Imagine! Sleeping alone. Alone in the dark!

"Nobody likes to sleep alone," said Anna's grandmother.

Anna Hibiscus laid her warm brown cheek on her mother's white arm. "Don't worry, Mama," she said. "You have all of us now. You will never be alone again."

But the next week, Anna's father said, "Anna Hibiscus, we are going on holiday. Your mother and myself with you and those brothers of yours. We will stay in a house on the beach."

"Only us?" asked Anna. This was incredible.

"Only us," said her father. "A quiet holiday."

Anna Hibiscus's mother smiled.

"But, Papa," asked Anna, "who is going to cook and shop and clean and ... everything? Who will take care of Double Trouble? What about me? Who will I play with?"

"I will help your mother to organize everything," Anna's father told her. "You, Anna Hibiscus, will take care of your brothers. You can play with them."

"But they are babies!" wailed Anna.

"Exactly!" said her father. "Now, enough problems. Let us pack."

One week later, Anna Hibiscus, her father,

her mother, Double and Trouble and all their boxes and bags crossed the road to the lagoon and squeezed themselves into a small canoe. The whole family waved them off.

"Don' stay away long!" they shouted. "Come home soon!"

The lagoon ran under and alongside busy roads and huge skyscrapers; it ran through markets bigger than towns. For the first time, Anna Hibiscus saw how big the city of Lagos was. It was gigantic.

Then it was gone.

Suddenly it was not buildings but trees that crowded the banks of the lagoon. Trees so tall and growing so thick together that Anna could not see into the dark rainforest. Only once did she see some people on the bank. They looked so tiny next to the tall trees.

Morning turned into afternoon turned into evening as they went slowly-slowly. Then Anna could see the island! A white sandy beach with small trees and, behind them, an open wooden house, painted white.

It was late by the time they got all their boxes and bags off the boat and up to the beach house. Anna Hibiscus's father lit lanterns and her mother warmed up food. They were all so tired from breathing sea breezes and carrying boxes and bags that they went straight to bed. Even Double and Trouble slept right through till morning.

When Anna and her family woke up, the beach house seemed dusty and dirty. It was full of cobwebs and dead cockroaches. Their boxes and bags were still packed. They were hungry. There was a lot to do.

After breakfast, Anna was put in charge of Double Trouble. They stayed downstairs on the veranda where it was cool and shady, but the boys kept crawling towards the edge. There were no doors for Anna to shut. She ran backwards and forwards grabbing each of her brothers in turn and putting him back in the middle of the room.

She was hot and sweating when at last she attached the boys to a table leg with her mother's scarf. They yelled and screamed. Anna's father came running.

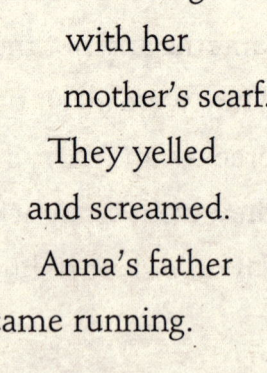

"Anna Hibiscus!" he said. "They are not goats!"

He untied them and watched them crawl quickly towards the edge of the veranda.

"I see." He sighed. "Double Trouble!"

He called to Anna's mother. "I'm taking Anna Hibiscus and Double Trouble to the beach. Where they cannot fall off any edge."

Anna's mother appeared in the kitchen doorway. There was a smudge on her face and cobwebs in her hair.

"OK," she sighed.

At the beach the boys wanted to crawl into the sea. The waves shot up their noses and splashed salt water in their eyes. They spluttered and choked and coughed.

Anna's father took them to play under the trees. "You go and splash yourself, Anna Hibiscus," he said. "I will stay here with your brothers."

Anna was not at all sure about splashing in the sea by herself. What if one of those big waves came along and drowned her? There would be no uncle or auntie to save her.

She put
one toe in the
water, but there were
no cousins to be brave with.

Anna Hibiscus could hear Double
and Trouble shouting and struggling.
They wanted to crawl back into the water.
They were not afraid.

Anna's father dug a big hole in the sand. Big enough for Double and Trouble to sit in and play. Too deep for the boys to climb out.

"You stay with them now, Anna," said her father. "I am going to swim."

Double and Trouble cried and screamed. They rubbed sand into their eyes and screamed louder. Anna sat with them in the hole. Her father's head looked like a ball in the waves.

A ball
getting smaller and smaller.
Just before it disappeared, it began to grow big again. Anna's father swam back with an idea.

He and Anna Hibiscus lifted the boys out of the hole and pointed them in the direction of the sea. Anna and her father ran down to the waves with Double Trouble crawling eagerly behind them.

They had time to splash and swim a little before the boys reached the water. Then Anna and her father helped them paddle before carrying them back up to the trees to start again. Double Trouble loved it! Anna Hibiscus and her father did this many, many, many times – until they were too tired to do it any more.

Back at the beach house, Anna Hibiscus's mother was tired too. She had swept up all the cockroaches. She had dusted away all the cobwebs. She had unpacked all the boxes and bags. She had walked all the way to the market to buy food, and walked all the way back. She had cooked the food.

Everybody was cross and tired. Everybody was hot and sticky. Everybody had a shower, ate food, and went to bed early. Everybody was asleep in one second.

Half an hour later, Double and Trouble woke up.

They were again hot and sticky. Their teeth were paining them. They were awake and angry. Anna Hibiscus's mother and father walked the baby boys up and down for hours while they screamed.

Anna Hibiscus lay in her bed. She had nobody to sleep with.

She missed her aunties. She missed how they took it in turns to rock sleepless babies. She missed how they sang and talked and made jokes and laughed no matter how loud the babies cried. Now Anna could hear only the waves and her brothers, screaming.

The next morning, Anna Hibiscus's father was so tired he could hardly speak. Anna Hibiscus's mother was so tired she cried. But the baby boys were full of life! They crawled everywhere, fast. Double pulled the tablecloth, and cups of tea spilt and rolled off the table onto the floor. Trouble crawled off the veranda and landed with a big bump on his head.

Anna's mother said, "I can't face it."

"You don't have to face it," Anna's father said. And he sent her back to bed.

He watched Anna trying to stop her brothers from crawling off the veranda. He remembered yesterday. He could not face it either.

Anna Hibiscus's father found the scarf and attached Double Trouble to the table leg. He set Anna to watch them.

"I go come," he said.

"Where?" asked Anna.

"I go to fetch aunties quick-quick," he said.

Anna Hibiscus smiled a big smile.

Later that morning, the aunties arrived. Six of them. They came with baskets of food. They came with little cousins who still needed them but no big cousins. They came with cuddles for Anna Hibiscus and many, many questions. When they saw Double and Trouble attached to the table leg they shouted and ran to loose them. Each boy was tied onto an auntie's back to keep him out of mischief. Then the aunties went into the kitchen and started to cook. Good smells spread all around, along with laughing and singing.

Anna's mother woke up. She stood blinking at the top of the stairs. She looked as if she did not know whether to laugh or to cry.

"Sister!" one of the aunties called. "Our brother confused your babies with the goats and tied them to the table!"

Anna's mother started to laugh *and* to cry. She came to greet the aunties. They embraced her.

"It is not good to be alone," Anna heard them whisper. "We have to help each other. A husband and three children is too much for one woman alone."

That night, everybody was happy.

The next day, the aunties and Anna Hibiscus's mother cooked and cleaned and washed clothes because they needed to. They splashed in the sea and sat talking on the beach because they were on holiday. They sang and joked because they were together.

And all the time, the little cousins were under their feet. Anna Hibiscus tried to play with them but they were babies and she could not look after them all. There were no big cousins to distract them, and no one else for them to follow around. The little cousins whined and howled. They grizzled and growled. Because that's what little children do. Anna Hibiscus was fed up with them.

By the end of the day, the aunties and Anna Hibiscus's mother were fed up with them too!

Back at the beach house they looked at Anna's father. "Today you sit down," they said. "Tomorrow you supervise this rabble!"

Anna Hibiscus's father looked at the rabble. He'd had a lovely quiet day eating the delicious food that the aunties had prepared and reading his newspapers. The rabble were snotty and sticky and cross. They scratched one another and pulled each other's hair.

"Tomorrow I will be here," he said. Then he quickly walked out of the house and disappeared down towards the beach.

Tomorrow he *was* there. He was there and all the big cousins that had been left behind were there to help him.

Anna's father supervised the big cousins supervising the little cousins over the top of his newspaper. The aunties and Anna's mother laughed and sighed and shook their heads.

Anna Hibiscus splashed and swam and ran and played with all her cousins. It was the best day so far.

That night, the women talked and joked together. The babies slept. The big cousins played their big-cousin games. Anna's father sat alone. He had no one to sit silently with, no one to smoke his pipe with. Anna came and laid her cheek on his knee.

"I am outnumbered, Anna Hibiscus," he said.

"You need the uncles," she said.

The next morning, the uncles were there! The aunties shrieked with surprise and laughed. Anna's father looked very pleased with himself. It was another good day and another good night.

But there came a day when everybody was annoyed and irritated. Nobody could agree. Anna's mother looked at Anna's father. He disappeared down towards the beach.

When he returned, Grandmother and Grandfather were with him. Grandmother and Grandfather had lived so long, they had become so wise and so calm that anybody who was with them was happy to accept their last word on everything. There was no need to quarrel. Harmony was restored.

Anna Hibiscus splashed in the sea with her big cousins; she chased her little cousins along the beach; she sang with her aunties and ate their good food; she laughed with her uncles and her father. She listened to Grandmother and Grandfather tell stories.

All together again, Anna Hibiscus's family had the happiest holiday they had ever had.

And Anna's mother? She had a very happy holiday too.

Auntie Comfort

Anna Hibiscus lives in Africa. Amazing Africa. In a country called Nigeria. Na-wa-oh Nigeria! She lives in a big white house with many rooms and balconies. She lives with her family, who do things the Nigerian way. Grandmother and Grandfather, who are very old and very wise, say it is important to do things the proper Nigerian way.

So all of Anna Hibiscus's family – her mother and her father, her aunties and her uncles, her cousins and Anna herself – bend their knees to Grandmother and Grandfather to show proper respect for their wisdom and

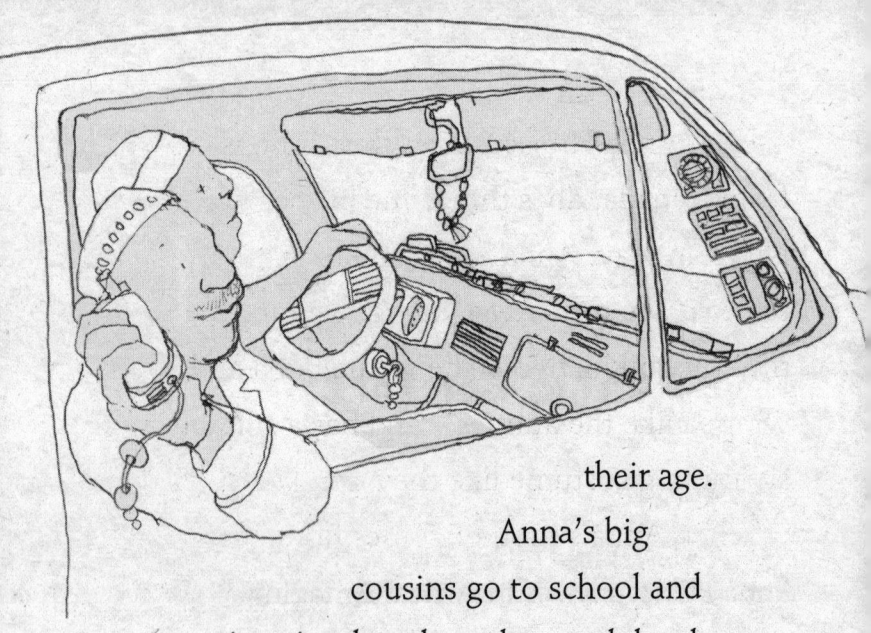

their age.

Anna's big cousins go to school and university, but they also work hard at home helping to wash the clothes, cook the food and look after the little cousins.

Anna's mother and father and aunties and uncles drive to work in their cars. They send text messages and emails around the world, and call from the market on their mobile phones to see what shopping needs doing. But the clothes they wear are made from colourful African cloth, waxed and dyed and printed. The languages they speak are Nigerian as well as English.

Even Anna Hibiscus's mother, who is from Canada, does things the proper Nigerian way. Anna has seen her in photos, when she was young, wearing a tiny-tiny bikini. Now she wears buba and wrappa like the aunties – and has a suitable swimming costume like they do.

When Anna's mother comes home from the office she pounds yam and cassava in the yard with the aunties. She cooks traditional food the traditional way – and she knows how to eat it properly with her fingers too!

You see, the whole family does things the proper African way, both modern and traditional. That is why Anna's grandmother and grandfather, her mother and her father, her aunties and her uncles, her cousins and her baby brothers – and Anna herself – all live together in the big white house.

All except for Auntie Comfort.

Auntie Comfort is one of Anna Hibiscus's favourite questions, especially on the Saturday Beach.

"Where is Auntie Comfort?"

"I've told you many, many times, Anna Hibiscus," her mother says, sighing.

"Tell me again, Mama, please," Anna begs.

"Again! Again!" all the little cousins shout.

And all the aunties sigh.

"You children will tire us!" they say.

But Uncle Tunde, who is not yet married and has no children and is not so tired of questions, says, "Auntie Comfort is in America."

"Where? Where?" Anna Hibiscus and all the little cousins shout.

Uncle Tunde points. "Over these same waves. On the other side of the Atlantic Ocean." He shades his eyes. "I can almost see her from here."

And they all jump up and try to see Auntie Comfort across the ocean.

Once, Anna was so excited she ran right down to the waves.

"Maybe one day, when you are strong enough," called Auntie Grace, "you will swim right across the Atlantic Ocean to Auntie Comfort!"

"Am I almost strong enough?" Anna Hibiscus said seriously.

Everybody laughed and laughed. And Anna didn't know why they were laughing at her. She wanted to cry.

"Come," said Anna's mother, who was in a good mood. "Let us send her a text message across the ocean instead!"

She showed Anna and the little cousins how to send a text message to Auntie Comfort. Anna pointed the mobile phone towards the waves and sent the message all the way across the Atlantic Ocean.

The next day was Sunday. On Sunday the whole family goes to church wearing special traditional clothes cut from the one same beautiful cloth to show they are all from the one same beautiful family.

Grandfather was proud of his family. He was happy that his sons were big and laughing. It pleased him that his daughters were strong and happy. He loved his grandchildren, full of life and trouble.

He looked at Grandmother, whose wise eyes were full of love, and he loved her too.

Only Comfort was missing. His youngest daughter. His comfort. Tears came suddenly into Grandfather's eyes. Anna Hibiscus, who was standing close to him, saw his tears. What could be troubling Grandfather? He was so old and so wise. Nothing should be allowed to trouble Grandfather! Anna Hibiscus went to him and put her hand in his.

The next day, a letter came. A letter from Auntie Comfort!

"Praise God!" said Grandfather when he had read it. "Comfort will visit us at last!"

Tears streamed down Grandmother and Grandfather's cheeks. Aunties and uncles and cousins jumped up and down, smiling and clapping and shouting, "Comfort is coming! Auntie Comfort is coming!"

"In three weeks' time," Grandfather continued, "Comfort will return on holiday."

And for three weeks everybody – little, medium and big – was busy working in preparation for Auntie Comfort's visit. When she came, every day would be a party.

Benz, Wonderful and all the big boy cousins led home from market goats carefully chosen by Grandfather and the uncles. They had to keep those goats tied up and eating.

Miracle, Sweetheart and all the little girl cousins were busy every day feeding the chickens fattening in pens.

The big gas stove in the kitchen was not big enough to prepare all the food.

Anna, Chocolate, Angel and all the medium-sized cousins were kept busy collecting wood to feed the fires. Pots bubbled and boiled and Anna's mother and aunties stirred and sweated and strained.

Joy, Clarity, Common Sense and all the big girl cousins grew muscles in their arms from pounding and pounding yam and cassava and millet.

Uncle Bizi Sunday, who did more shopping and cooking than anyone else, did not sleep – not at all.

Soon the big fridges and freezers were stuffed full of delicious food and soft drinks, all waiting for Auntie Comfort to arrive.

But every evening when the family gathered to eat, a tear would run down Grandfather's cheek. He would look around at his wife and children and grandchildren, all rolling balls of yam neatly between their fingertips and popping them in their mouths.

"Will Comfort remember how to eat?" he would say. "Will she remember our way? The proper Nigerian way? Will she have forgotten her fingers and know only knife and fork now?"

The aunties and uncles would look at one another and smile and shrug their shoulders. They did not know. Only Anna Hibiscus was worried that Grandfather was sad again.

One night she asked her mother, "Mama, can I send a message on your phone?"

"What are you talking about, Anna Hibiscus?" her mother said, cross and tired. "To who? Mobile phones are not for small-small children."

Uncle Tunde heard. He saw Anna's tears. Uncle Tunde did not have small-small children and he was not so tired.

"Don't worry, Anna Hibiscus," he said. "You can use my phone."

So Anna sent a message across the Atlantic Ocean and only Uncle Tunde knew.

In those three weeks before Auntie Comfort came, much new cloth was bought and new clothes made for the whole family. A lot of text messages were sent back and forth between the cloth market and the house. Auntie Comfort emailed her measurements and the tailor came on his bicycle, his sewing machine strapped on the back, to help with the making of the new clothes.

Grandmother called Grandfather to inspect each fitting.

Grandfather sighed and shook his head when they held up Auntie Comfort's new clothes. "But will Comfort even know how to tie wrappa any more? The proper Nigerian way? Maybe she will only wear tight-tight jean now."

Angel and Chocolate and Anna Hibiscus looked at one another with eyes wide open. An auntie wearing tight-tight jean! The boy cousins giggled. The uncles laughed. Grandmother looked worried.

Anna Hibiscus borrowed Uncle Tunde's phone again.

The three weeks were almost gone. Anna was excited. Whenever she could she ran off to play at being Auntie Comfort. Auntie Comfort in the office with many secretaries sending important emails and faxes around the world. All the cousins loved to play this game. On the last day they played Auntie Comfort shopping for their presents!

Grandfather came out to watch. He shook his head.

"It is the proper Nigerian way to bring gifts for everyone," he said. "Maybe Auntie Comfort will not remember."

The cousins looked at one another. Now they were *all* worried.

Anna Hibiscus went running to Uncle Tunde. But it was too late! Too late for Auntie Comfort to go shopping – Auntie Comfort was coming tomorrow!

The next day, Anna Hibiscus's father and Uncle Tunde drove to the airport to collect Auntie Comfort.

The family stood on the porch in their new clothes. They watched and they waited.

When Anna's father and Uncle Tunde returned they were smiling from ear to ear. And when Auntie Comfort stepped out of the car everybody gasped.

Auntie Comfort was wearing the biggest, longest, fullest, stiffest traditional dress that Anna and her cousins had ever seen. It was a miracle that her head tie had fitted inside the car!

Auntie Comfort looked like a queen. The Queen of Nigeria! Uncle Tunde winked at Anna Hibiscus.

When Auntie Comfort knelt in front of Grandmother and Grandfather, Anna Hibiscus thought she was the finest queen Anna had ever seen.

Anna's mother and all the aunties were crying with joy and relief. Anna's father and the uncles were laughing and smiling. Grandfather's smile was the happiest smile of all. And Anna Hibiscus's was the widest.

"Welcome, Comfort!" Grandfather said.

"Thank you, Father," Auntie Comfort replied. "But I am now called Yemisi."

"Why?" said Grandmother. "What is wrong with Comfort?"

"I wanted to have a Nigerian name, Mama," said Auntie Comfort.

The aunties started to laugh.

"Comfort is a Nigerian name," said Grandmother.

"But it is an English word, Mama," said Auntie Comfort.

"It is an English word, but a Nigerian name," said Grandfather. "Have you ever heard of any English person being called Comfort? Come, enough of this. Let us eat."

The table had been laid according to Grandfather's instructions. There were plates at every place, and many knives and forks and spoons, for the many courses. They ate pepper soup with their spoons and then eba and okro and stew were served. Everybody looked at Auntie Comfort. Auntie Comfort looked politely at Grandmother and Grandfather.

Grandfather gestured to Auntie Comfort. "Begin, my daughter," he said.

Auntie Comfort motioned for the finger-washing bowl to be passed to her. Then she began. Rolling the eba into neat little balls with her fingertips, dipping it into the okro and stew and then popping it into her mouth.

The cousins clapped and clapped. Big fat happy tears ran down the cheeks of Grandmother and Grandfather. Auntie Comfort looked surprised … and then she winked at Anna Hibiscus. Anna Hibiscus smiled her biggest smile.

The worry was over. Except …

... what was inside Auntie Comfort's many big suitcases? Presents, of course!
There were presents for Grandmother and Grandfather, for Mother and Father and all the aunties and uncles, *and* there were presents for Anna, Double Trouble, Benz, Wonderful, Miracle, Sweetheart, Chocolate, Angel, Joy, Clarity, Common Sense and all of the cousins. Everybody cried with excitement and hugged Auntie Comfort over and over again. Nobody had been forgotten! Not the neighbours, not the distant relatives, not the girls who

stood selling fruit and vegetables at the gate. Nobody.

Anna was delighted. Auntie Comfort had thought of everything and everyone.

After that, everybody, including Anna Hibiscus, knew that Auntie Comfort was still a true and proper Nigerian lady, both modern and traditional.

"Our daughter has come," Grandmother said over and over again.

"Our daughter has not only come," Grandfather said, "she has also remained one of us."

And everybody agreed.

Lucky, though, thought Anna Hibiscus
when Auntie Comfort went splashing
in the waves in a tiny-tiny bikini,
lucky Grandmother and Grandfather
don't come to the beach!

Anna Hibiscus sells oranges

Anna Hibiscus lives in Africa. Amazing
Africa. In a country called Nigeria.
Na-wa-oh Nigeria! She and her family live
in a big white house in a beautiful garden.
All around the compound is a wide white
wall. Outside the wall is the city of Lagos.

Lagos is a big African city of lagoons and bridges and roads, of skyscrapers and shanty towns. Ships and boats sail up and down the lagoons, which wind through the city from the sea to the rainforest. Ships and boats loaded with people and goats and goods. Every road is jammed with hundreds and thousands of cars, buses, taxis and motorbikes, all loaded with people and all blowing their horns.

There are millions and millions of people in Anna Hibiscus's city: people being born and people dying, people growing up and people growing old, people studying and people working, working, working. People walking, running, driving; singing, talking, shouting; laughing and fighting; buying and selling. The city is always busy and noisy and loud.

But, however noisy the city was, inside Anna Hibiscus's compound it was quiet, quiet, quiet. Auntie Comfort had flown back across the Atlantic Ocean to America. The days-long parties were over. The distant relatives had returned to their villages and the neighbours had gone home. The big cousins were at school and aunties and uncles were at work.

There were now only the daytime sounds of little cousins playing and a few aunties, sometimes singing, sometimes scolding. There were now only the evening sounds of uncles laughing and discussing. Sometimes only the murmur of Grandmother and Grandfather's soft words could be heard.

Anna Hibiscus was bored of this quiet. She was bored of playing with her cousins; bored of housework with her mother; bored of listening quietly to Grandmother and Grandfather.

Anna loved to stand at the gate and watch the city. She knew all the girls who stood outside the gate selling fruit and vegetables from baskets piled high on their heads. She knew the women who squatted in the road frying plantains and plaiting hair for money. She knew the small boys who sold matches. They all called and sang to the people passing on foot, or in cars and buses and bikes: "COME AN' BUY! COME AN' BUY!"

Anna loved the girls who sold oranges and plantains the most. Whole busloads of people stopped to buy their oranges. Motorbikes pulled over for plantains. Those girls shouted and screamed and laughed and talked to everybody. They ran after passing cars for money held out of opened windows. They fought off goats who ate the 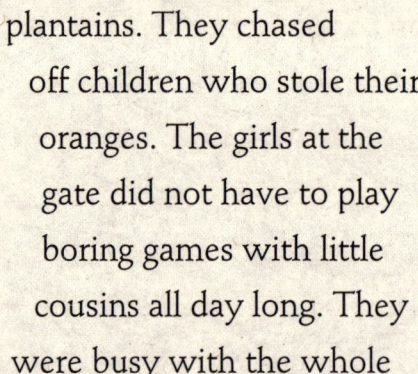 plantains. They chased off children who stole their oranges. The girls at the gate did not have to play boring games with little cousins all day long. They were busy with the whole city. Those girls did not look bored.

Many, many times Anna Hibiscus
asked her mother and her father,
her grandmother and her
grandfather, "*Abeg*, Papa,
please can I go out? I
want to sell oranges
at the gate."

But Grandfather
always laughed.

"Ah-ah, Anna
Hibiscus, why do you
want to sell oranges?
You are a lucky girl.
You have a father and a
mother who work for you.
Even I, when I was young, worked
for you: for our beautiful big white house,
for our garden where you can play and pick
fruit any time you like. Go and play, Anna
Hibiscus; you do not know how lucky
you are!"

But one day Anna Hibiscus was so bored she decided not to listen to Grandfather. She decided to sell oranges anyway.

Anna found a big basket. She climbed one of the orange trees and filled it full of fruit. Then she slipped out of the gate with her basket on her head.

"Orrrr-enge! Orrrr-enge!"

Anna Hibiscus shouted just like the other girls. They all looked at her with surprised and worried eyes.

Anna Hibiscus's oranges were bright and clean and shiny. They were fresh off the tree. The other girls' oranges were dusty and soft.

Their oranges had travelled
in lorries along bumpy
dry roads all the way
from the orange
farms to the
city. Their
oranges had
sat in the
sun in dirty
markets. Their
oranges had been carried
in open baskets along polluted roads. Their
oranges were small and orange-brown.

The girls' dresses were faded and torn.
But Anna Hibiscus was as bright and clean
and shiny as her oranges. All the people
who stopped wanted the big bright oranges
from the smart little girl. Anna sold all her
oranges. She filled up her basket again and
again and sold them all. The other girls sold
almost none that day.

Anna Hibiscus was so excited. As evening fell she rushed back through the gate and into the house. He smile was as bright and shining as the money in her pocket.

But when Anna's father and uncles came home from work they looked worried.

"Something happen to those girls at the gate today. Some kind of trouble," the eldest uncle said. "That Angelina, with no mother, no father, only one sick brother at home. Angelina always smiles. Today she cries."

"Is true," said Uncle Tunde. "And Bola, with her polio-shrivelled legs, who has to work morning and night for food. She crying too."

"Yes," said Anna's father. "And Hasa with twelve brother-sisters, whose father has died, why is she so sad today?"

The big bright smile fell off Anna Hibiscus's face.

Grandfather was worried. What had

happened to trouble the poor girls so?
He went himself to the gate but the
girls had all gone.

Anna came and stood beside
her grandfather. They looked
at the yellow lights and the
hustle of the city. Anna held
out her hand. The coins
were shining on her palm.

"What is this, Anna
Hibiscus?" her grandfather
asked.

"I sold our oranges, Grandfather," she
whispered. "Now the girls have no money
for food for their little brothers and sisters…"

Anna started to cry. Grandfather looked
up at the empty orange trees. He looked
down at his crying granddaughter.

"People will be hungry tonight, Anna
Hibiscus, because of what you have done."

Anna hid alone in her room and cried.

Early the next morning, Grandfather called her. "Come, Anna Hibiscus, bring your basket."

Slowly Anna followed her grandfather to the gate. The girls were already there, desperate to sell their oranges and plantains.

"Today my granddaughter will work for you," Grandfather said. "Today she will collect oranges from the market and bring them here. You will not have to walk back and forth in the heat every time your basket is empty. Today you will be able to sell many, many oranges."

Grandfather led Anna Hibiscus along the road to the market. It was a long way. There was no shade; there was no cool grass; there was no pavement. On one side of Anna was the gutter with its old green stinking water. On the other side was the traffic – loud horns blasting, engines roaring, exhaust fumes belching. Anna Hibiscus and her grandfather went slowly because they were an old man and a small girl unused to walking to market. All the other people jostled and pushed past them. Sweat poured down Anna's face and into her eyes. Her throat burned with dust and car fumes.

At last they reached the place where the market women haggled and screamed. Grandfather led the way to the fruit sellers. He filled Anna's basket with the best oranges. The bright coins from yesterday were still in Anna's pocket. She took them out and gave them to the orange seller.

Back and forth they went. Back and forth. Sweat stained Grandfather's shirt. He leant heavily on his cane. Grandfather was too old to walk back and

forth in the hot busy city.

"Maybe Mama or Auntie or Uncle could walk with me, Grandfather," Anna said.

"They are all busy with their work," Grandfather said. "I will not give them more."

Tears poured quietly down Anna Hibiscus's face.

When afternoon came, Grandfather went to rest and Grandmother joined Anna Hibiscus. Anna walked on and on, the heavy orange basket on her head. She did not stop. Not once.

When night fell, Grandfather was

waiting for Anna at the gate. The girls were there too. Everybody had big smiles on their faces.

"This one small girl work hard-o!" the gate girls cried.

"Carry enough orange for all of us to sell plenty-plenty!"

"Well done-o! Well done!"

Grandfather led Anna Hibiscus into the compound. Her feet had blisters, her head was aching and her legs were sore. Her ears were ringing from the car horns. Her throat and eyes were stinging with sweat and dust and fumes. But Anna was smiling too.

"Grandfather, send her to work again-o!" called the girls.

Anna Hibiscus's grandfather laughed.

"Now Anna knows what it is to work hard," he said. "Maybe now she won't be so bored of the peace and quiet."

sweet snow

Anna Hibiscus lives in Africa. Amazing Africa. In a country called Nigeria. Na-wa-oh Nigeria! And because of this, Anna Hibiscus has never once seen snow. More than anything else in the entire world Anna longs to set her eyes, her feet, her hands, on snow.

Anna Hibiscus lives in a wonderful house with many, many rooms and balconies. But more wonderful than this, more wonderful than anything else in the entire world, so Anna thinks, is snow.

All day long Anna Hibiscus plays in the garden around the house. A garden full of cool grass to lie on, beautiful trees to climb up and lovely flowers to smell. The trees are full of sweet fruit and the flowers are full of sweet nectar. But nothing can be sweet like snow, Anna has decided; nothing can be so cool.

Anna Hibiscus lives with her mother
and her father, her grandmother and her
grandfather, her aunties and her uncles,
her cousins and her brothers, Double
and Trouble. Anna Hibiscus's family
is so big she cannot count them all. But
nothing is more unaccountable than snow,
Anna thinks.

One morning, in the amazing land of
Africa, in the wonderful house with the
wonderful garden, Anna Hibiscus woke
up and her room was white. Floating white.

"SNOW!" shouted Anna.

Anna's cousins Chocolate and Angel
woke up. Anna was waving her arms,
and the breeze from the air conditioner
that cooled down the hot Nigerian air
was floating white all about her. There
were Double and Trouble sitting on
the floor, feathers round their mouths,
chewing Chocolate's pillow.

"Snowing feathers!"
Angel cried, and she
shook her pillow.

Now Anna Hibiscus can think of nothing but snow. Snow! Snow! Snow! She and her cousins played snowstorms howling down corridors. They stormed through the rooms until their mothers chased them out into the garden.

Anna climbed the big mango tree where her big boy cousins were sitting, eating mangoes.

"This one's sweet-o," shouted Anna, biting into a ripe one.

"But not sweet like snow-o. You agree, cousin Benz? You agree, cousin Wonderful? Nothing's sweet like snow!"

Anna Hibiscus talked on and on until the boy cousins shook the branches of the tree and she almost fell out.

She climbed down shouting, "Just because you no know snow!"

It was true. Her cousins knew nothing about snow, her father knew nothing about snow, her grandfather and her grandmother knew nothing about snow, her aunties and her uncles knew nothing about snow, even Anna Hibiscus herself did not know snow. Nobody in Anna's family knew anything about snow because nobody in Anna's family had ever, even once, seen snow. Nobody except for Anna Hibiscus's mother.

You see, a long time ago, before Anna Hibiscus was born, when her father was a young man, he had gone to a country called Canada. He had gone in the short summertime and there he had met Anna's mother.

They had got married and come quickly back to Africa before the long winter came and Anna's father got too cold.

So Anna's mother knew all about snow. She had been born during a snowstorm and had grown up building snowmen and throwing snowballs. She had sledged and tobogganed over mountains of snow. She had even skied across snow-covered fields to school.

But Anna knew better than to ask about snow again, now, today, when her mother and the aunties were busy in the house.

So Anna Hibiscus went to the gate, but everybody outside was quick and shout and hurry today: buying and selling, haggling and screaming, walking and rushing; *quick* and *shout* and *hurry!* Nobody wanted to stop and talk to Anna except for a small beggar boy. Anna gave him the mango she had in her pocket. She started to tell him about snow – like cassava flakes falling from the sky!

"You de craze," the beggar boy said and ran away.

"I no de craze!" Anna shouted.

She ran to tell Grandmother.

"It is not kind to talk of cassava falling from the sky to somebody who is always hungry," her grandmother said.

"You were mean, Anna!" whispered her cousin Chocolate.

Anna Hibiscus was cross. She went into the kitchen. Uncle Bizi Sunday would be there and he would be nice to her. He was the chief of the shopping and the cooking. And he was often in the kitchen, commanding and organizing it all.

When Anna Hibiscus came in, Uncle Bizi Sunday was measuring rice. Anna watched the small white grains being scooped up from the sack and falling into the bowl.

"Snow is like rice, Uncle," said Anna. She knew he would not say she was crazy. "Like rice falling from the sky," she said.

Anna reached for some rice to show him how it could fall from the sky, but Uncle Bizi Sunday closed the sack.

"Finish," he said.

"Oh," said Anna Hibiscus. "Well, rice is not so much

like snow. Snow is cold." She looked around and saw the big freezer. "Cold like ice," she said.

Anna Hibiscus opened the freezer. It was cold and soft inside. She scraped out handfuls of ice and threw them into the air.

"Look, Uncle!" she said. "Look at the snow!"

Ice flew into the air and fell onto the floor. It melted into puddles.

Uncle Bizi Sunday looked at the puddles. "Overseas it snows," he said.

"Yes, Uncle, in Scotland and Alaska and Iceland and Canada," said Anna Hibiscus.

"It snows in kitchens?" asked Uncle Bizi Sunday.

"No, Uncle," said Anna slowly. "It snows outside."

"So why is there snow in my kitchen?"
Uncle Bizi Sunday was aggravated.
  Anna hurried to mop up the puddles.

Her mother came in while Anna was mopping.

"Anna! I have been looking for you," she said. "Here is a letter from Granny Canada! How would you like to visit her next summer? She will buy you a ticket on the aeroplane!"

Anna Hibiscus stood still as a stone. Only her eyes grew wider and wider.

Suddenly she leapt into the air and shrieked like a peacock.

"SNOW!"

Anna Hibiscus sang, waving the mop:

"Snow, you are wonderful!
I will see and tell you so!
Snow, you are so cold-o!
I will feel and say you so!
Snow, you are so sweet-o!
I will taste and tell you so!
SNOW—"

"Anna!" her mother interrupted gently. "There is no snow in the summertime."

Anna Hibiscus stopped dancing. Her eyes grew full of tears. Uncle Bizi Sunday came to stand beside her. "This child has to see snow," he said.

Somewhere inside the house Double and Trouble started to cry. They cried and cried and cried. Nobody was picking them up.

Anna's mother turned to go. "I just don't know," she said.

Anna sat down on the floor and her tears splash, splash, splashed into a puddle. Uncle Bizi Sunday hurried out of the kitchen. When he came back he was carrying paper and an envelope. He took a pen from a drawer.

"Anna Hibiscus," he said. "Come! You must write."

"Why?" Anna wailed.

"You must write to Granny Canada – tell her you love snow."

Anna stopped crying. She looked at Uncle Bizi Sunday.

"Come," he said. "You write. I post."

Uncle Bizi Sunday wiped away Anna's tears and sat her on a stool to write.

> Dear Granny Canada,
> Thank you for inviting me.
> I want to see you and Canada and
> the bears and go on the aeroplane.
> But I wish I could see snow too.
> I really really really love snow.
> Love from Anna Hibiscus

Anna put the letter in the envelope and stuck it down.

"The address!" she wailed.

"I know it," Uncle Bizi Sunday said. "Your mama told me one time."

Uncle Bizi Sunday had never been to school. He could not read; he could not write. But he could remember everything he was told. Even if he only heard it one time.

He said the address carefully and Anna copied it down. The letter was ready! Uncle Bizi Sunday readied himself. He took off his apron and put on his shirt. He put the letter in his pocket.

Anna Hibiscus watched him walk to the gate. She saw him stop and count the coins in his pocket before he went out. Then he was gone.

Anna Hibiscus waited while Uncle Bizi Sunday took the letter to the post office. Had she spelt the address right? Anna Hibiscus crossed her fingers. She waited a long, long time while the letter was sitting in the post office until an aeroplane flew it all the way across Africa, and over the ocean to where her granny lived in Canada. She waited while the postman in Canada slowly read the address and then

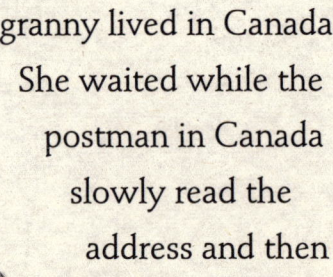

delivered the letter to her granny. She waited while her granny opened the letter, read it and smiled. She waited while her granny wrote a letter back and that new letter flew all the way across the ocean, and all the way across Africa to where Anna Hibiscus lived. Anna Hibiscus waited for weeks for that letter, while her fingers remained crossed.

Then one day, as Anna was sitting in the big mango tree with her cousins, somebody shouted,
"A letter! A letter for Anna Hibiscus!"

Anna almost fell out of the tree, again. Everybody in Anna's family came running. Her father, her grandfather, her grandmother, her uncles, her aunties; all of her cousins; her mother with her two baby brothers; but first and fastest was Uncle Bizi Sunday.

"A letter from Canada!" Chocolate shouted, looking at the stamp. "Read, Anna! Read!"

> Dear Anna Hibiscus,
> Why don't you come and visit me at Christmas time instead? Then there will be plenty of snow for you to see. I would love to have you to stay for Christmas. See what your parents say.
> Love Granny Canada

Anna Hibiscus took a deep breath. She looked up at her mother and her father. Her father was looking at her mother. Her mother was looking at her.

"Anna Hibiscus?" her mother said.

"I wrote to Granny Canada," Anna said. "I wrote that I love snow."

Her mother opened her mouth, but before she could speak: "Initiative!" said Grandfather. "Can she go?"

"Of course," her father said. "Of course you can go, Anna Hibiscus."

Anna could not move. Christmas time. Here the trees would be covered with leaves and lights and her family would be dancing to music beneath them. The days would be long and warm. But she, Anna Hibiscus, would be where the trees were bare. The days would be short and cold and she would play in …

"SNOW!" shouted Anna.

Everybody cheered and clapped and laughed. Chocolate and Angel sang. Uncle Bizi Sunday danced Anna Hibiscus around and around. Hip-hip …

HOORAY!

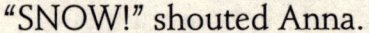

"Snow, you are wonderful!
Anna will see and tell you so!
Snow, you are so cold-o!
Anna will feel and say you so!
Snow, you are so sweet-o!
Anna will taste and tell us so!
SNOW!"

Hooray for ANNA HIBISCUS!

by Atinuke
illustrated by Lauren Tobia

WALKER BOOKS

To my sisters,
OE and TJ, the original
Double and Trouble
A.

To all the babies,
Hannah, Max, Billy, Finn,
Niamh and Ciara
L.T.

Anna 'biscus! Sing!

Anna Hibiscus lives in Africa. Amazing Africa. In a country called Nigeria. Na-wa-oh Nigeria! She lives with her mother and her father; her grandmother and her grandfather; her aunties and her uncles; her cousins, little, medium and big; and her twin baby brothers, Double and Trouble. They all live together in a big white house in the city of Lagos.

Anna Hibiscus stays at home all day long with the little cousins. Little cousins do

not go to school. They help their mothers and aunties with the work of the big white house and they play in the beautiful flower-filled garden.

Anna Hibiscus loves helping her mother and her aunties wash clothes. She loves feeding the chickens and climbing the mango trees to pick the sweet fruit. But especially and particularly Anna Hibiscus loves singing. She loves singing to her brothers, Double and Trouble, all day long.

Double and Trouble are still babies, they are only just now saying something. They have three new words that Anna Hibiscus is always listening out for.

Trouble's two words are "Anna 'biscus!"

And Double's word is "Sing!"

And if ever they are confused, if ever they are bored or tired, Double and Trouble shout:

"Anna 'biscus!"

"Sing!"

And Anna comes running from wherever she is to sing to her brothers. Because Anna Hibiscus loves her brothers, and Anna Hibiscus loves to sing.

This Christmas, for the very first time, Anna Hibiscus will see snow – in Canada! So she sings about snow:

> "Snow, you are wonderful!
> I will see and tell you so!
> Snow, you are so cold-o!
> I will feel and say you so!
> Snow, you are so sweet-o!
> I will taste and tell you so!"

All day long while Anna is singing and playing at home, her father and the uncles and some of the aunties are working hard in their offices and businesses and churches to make Nigeria a Better Place.

One day Anna Hibiscus's father came home from work. "I want to talk to you, Anna Hibiscus," he said. "I need to explain something important. You are still small but you are growing bigger every day. You are growing up! And growing-up children have work to do. Work to make Nigeria – and the whole entire world – a Better Place."

"What work, Papa?" Anna Hibiscus asked.

"It is this," Anna Hibiscus's father said. "Now you are growing up you must go to school."

Anna Hibiscus was sad. She did not want to go to school where she knew nobody and nobody knew her (except for a few cousins). She did not want to leave the big white house.

But the next school day, her mother came to call her and Anna Hibiscus was very brave. She got up early and put on a clean school uniform that used to belong to her big cousin Clarity and said goodbye to Grandmother and Grandfather and her mother and her father and the aunties and the uncles and the little cousins and the chickens and the goats and the mango trees and the big white house and the beautiful garden and Double Trouble, and squeezed into the car with all the other growing-up cousins and went to school.

All morning while she was at school, Anna Hibiscus missed everybody and everything in the big white house and the beautiful wide compound. But most especially and enormously she missed Double Trouble. She was so far away she could not hear them say, "Anna 'biscus! Sing!" So every outside break time Anna Hibiscus sang as loudly as she could in the direction of the big white house just in case they could hear her.

One night when Anna Hibiscus's mother and father and aunties and uncles came back from their work, they were full of talk. They called all the cousins and the stay-at-home aunties and uncles and Grandmother and Grandfather and told everybody that for the very first time the president of a country outside of Africa was coming to visit their own country.

"Ours is only one of many countries in Africa," began Uncle Tunde.

"We must show this president how wonderful our country is," Auntie Joly said.

"And how important things are here," Anna's father added.

"But most important of all," Grandfather said gently, "this president will be our guest. We must make sure she is comfortable and at ease."

"Then, when she goes away," Grandmother said, "she will have only kind-hearted feelings towards our country and our people."

And everybody agreed.

At school the next day, everybody was talking about the same thing.

Anna Hibiscus's teacher announced, "There will be a big welcoming ceremony in the National Stadium for the visiting president. Our school has been asked to participate. We must send a good speaker, a good dancer and a good singer."

She chose a good speaker and a good dancer, and then she said, "Hands up who can sing."

Many children's hands went up. They all wanted to sing in the National Stadium for the important president. Anna Hibiscus sat on her hands. She did not want to sing in

front of the president. What if she did not like Anna's song? Then she would go away with no good feelings for Anna's country. And it would all be the fault of Anna Hibiscus and her useless song.

The teacher looked at the children. She had never heard them sing. She did not know who to pick.

Then Anna's cousin Angel said, "Anna Hibiscus can sing!"

"Yes! Yes!" everybody shouted. "It is true! It is true! Anna Hibiscus is singing all the time."

The teacher made Anna Hibiscus stand up. "Sing, Anna," she said.

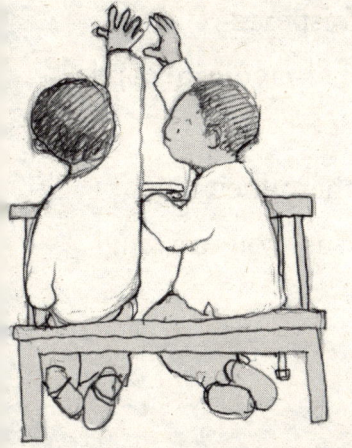

Anna Hibiscus stood up. She did not know what to sing.

"Sing 'Snow'," Angel whispered.

So Anna Hibiscus sang her favourite song about snow.

"It is true," said the teacher when Anna had finished. "Anna Hibiscus, you can sing! We will send you!"

Back at the big white house, Chocolate and Angel told everybody, "Anna Hibiscus is going to sing for the visiting president!"

"What is this?" everybody asked Anna.

"It is true," Anna Hibiscus said. "My school is going to send me to sing for the president."

"At the National Stadium!" said Chocolate.

"She is going to sing all on her own!" said Angel.

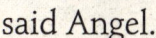

Anna Hibiscus felt very sorry for herself. Double and Trouble looked at her worried face. They felt worried too. "Anna 'biscus! Sing! Anna 'biscus! Sing!" they shouted.

So Anna Hibiscus sang for them until she felt much better.

And now Anna did not mind going to school so much. She did not do mathematics or spelling any more. She only sang and sang and sang her new president song!

And in the afternoon when she got home, Double Trouble shouted, "Anna 'biscus! Anna 'biscus! Sing! Sing!"

And Anna Hibiscus sang her new president song.

And at night when Double and Trouble went to bed, Anna Hibiscus sang it to them again. It was their new favourite song!

"Welcome to our beautiful country,
Welcome to our wonderful land.
Welcome to the sun shining brightly,
Welcome to our cool evening rain…"

Morning, noon and night, Anna Hibiscus sang this song. She did not tire of singing it. It was *her* new favourite song too.

Anna Hibiscus was happy singing at school and at home. But one day she went to practise at the National Stadium and then she was not happy any more. The stage was as big as a football pitch. There were thousands of seats in front and all around. Anna felt very small on that stage. She felt as small as an ant. An ant standing alone under World Cup lights.

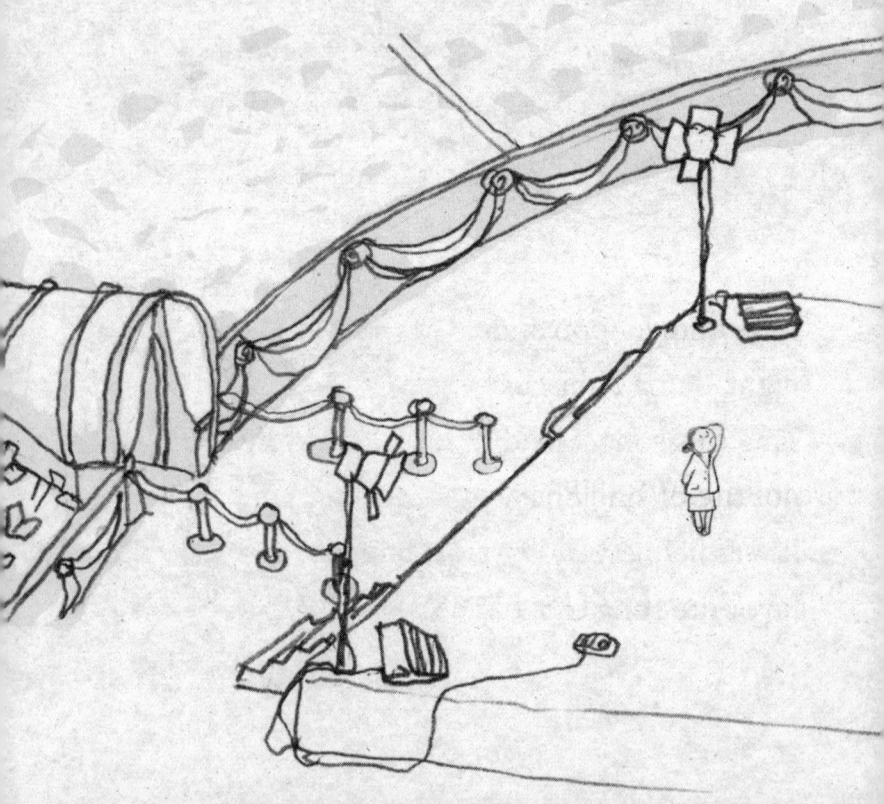

"Don't worry," said Chocolate when Anna came home, "we will be there. It will be us sitting there. Don't be afraid."

"Don't worry," said Angel. "You know you can sing. We all know you can sing."

"Sing! Sing!" said Double happily, and Trouble clapped his hands.

On the night the president arrived, everybody in Anna Hibiscus's family was there waiting at the National Stadium. Her mother and her father and all of their friends. Her grandmother and her grandfather and all of their friends. Her aunties and her uncles and all of their friends. Her cousins, little, medium and big, and all of their friends! Even Double and Trouble were there. They were noisy babies who were meant to be left at home, but they cried so much at being left behind that Anna's mother and father took pity on them and brought them along too.

Up on the stage many adults and children made long speeches of welcome. Traditional dances were performed by many schools. The big national choir sang welcome songs.

Then it was the turn of Anna Hibiscus.

Anna stood alone on the stage. On a stage big enough for a football match

Anna Hibiscus stood alone. A sea of faces rose in front of her but the lights shone in her eyes and she could not see one face she knew. There was nobody standing beside her or behind her. Nobody to hold her hand or sing with her. There were only all those people looking at her; and one of those people, Anna knew, was a president from a strange and faraway country.

Anna Hibiscus forgot her song.

The audience was silent. Everybody was waiting for the small girl on stage to speak or sing or dance or do something. The visiting president looked at her watch.

Anna Hibiscus did nothing. She did not know her song any more. Her throat was a dry riverbed. Her bones had turned to stone. She could not move. Not even to run off the stage.

Anna Hibiscus's mother and father, grandmother and grandfather, aunties and uncles, cousins and friends all looked at one another. They held their breath and waited.

And waited.

Double was bored. He climbed up on his chair. Trouble was bored. He too stood up on his chair. Anna's mother and the aunties struggled to make them sit down. Double and Trouble could see Anna Hibiscus standing there on the stage alone. Double and Trouble were confused. They were bored. They were tired. There was only one thing to do.

"Anna 'biscus!" Trouble shouted.
"Sing!" shouted Double.

Alone on the stage Anna Hibiscus heard the brothers she loved shout. She looked up, and there they were! Out in the audience, above everybody else!

Suddenly Anna Hibiscus was not alone. Her bones came alive. Her throat was no longer dry. She remembered her song! It ran like a river! Anna opened her mouth and sang!

"Welcome to our beautiful country,
Welcome to our wonderful land.
Welcome to the sun shining brightly,
Welcome to our cool evening rain.
Welcome to our flowers always blooming,
Welcome to our trees always green.
Welcome to our rivers of fishes,
Welcome to our farms growing food.
Welcome to our deep dark rainforest,
Welcome to our industries sound.
Welcome to our schools full of children,
Welcome to our cities and towns.
Welcome to our beautiful country,
Welcome to our sweet motherland!"

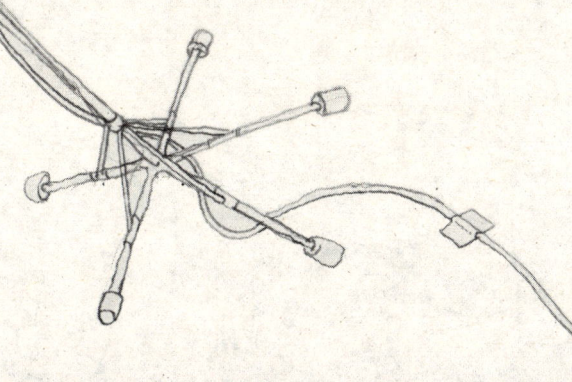

The audience clapped and clapped and clapped. The foreign president stood up on her feet and clapped. Anna's family and friends stood up on their feet and clapped. Everybody stood up and clapped.

"Hooray!" shouted Grandfather.

"Hooray!" shouted Grandmother.

"Hooray!" shouted her mother and father and aunties and uncles and cousins and friends and everybody else.

"Hooray! Anna 'biscus!" shouted Trouble.

"Anna 'biscus! Hooray!" shouted Double.

They were clapping the longest and shouting the loudest.
Hooray! Hooray! Hooray!
It was their new favourite word.

Your Hair, Anna Hibiscus!

Anna Hibiscus lives with her whole
entire family in Africa. Wonderful Africa.
Amazing Africa. Africa, where girls have
beautiful hair. Short or long, the hair of an
African girl is thicker and shinier and curlier
than any other hair in the whole world.

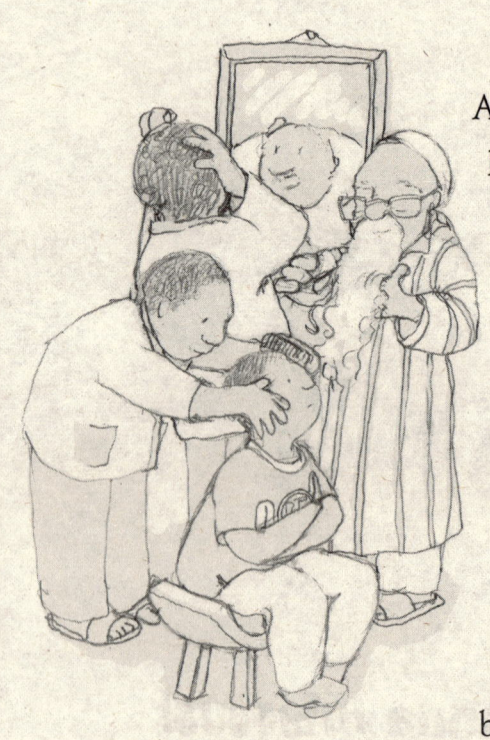

Everybody in Anna's family must look after their hair. They must oil it so that it shines and sparkles in the sunlight. They must comb it well-well.

Anna's grandfather, father, uncles and boy cousins have short-short hair. Oil, comb, and the palaver is over. Not so for Anna Hibiscus and her girl cousins with their long-long hair. Not so for her aunties. For them the headache has only just begun.

Grandmother and Grandfather say it is best to observe the traditional Nigerian ways and the whole family agree.

Traditional Nigerian women
and girls plait and braid their hair.
That is how such thick and
curly hair stays shiny
and beautiful and neat
with no chemicals
whatsoever.

But Anna Hibiscus knows
that plaiting and weaving mean hours and
hours of hair-pulling and head-squeezing
and scalp-yanking.

Anna Hibiscus hates her hair. It is too thick; it is too curly. Never mind that it is beautiful and shiny. Anna Hibiscus *hates* it.

And one day Anna Hibiscus decides she cannot stand looking after it any more.

It was one Friday evening. Anna Hibiscus was sitting on the floor while her cousin Joy loosened all her tiny-tiny plaits. Anna was uncomfortable; Anna was bored; Anna was cross. Every Friday evening was the same. Pull! Tug! Yank! The plaits that had been holding her thick hair tight and neat all week had to be loosened ready to be weaved tight and neat again the next day.

All around the room, Grandmother was helping aunties, aunties were helping big girl cousins, and big girl cousins were helping little girl cousins to loosen all the tiny tiny tight-tight plaits on each others' heads.

Anna's head was pulled first one way and then the other. She was getting crosser and more uncomfortable but she did not dare complain.

"Do you see anybody else complaining?" her aunties would ask.

Anna Hibiscus did not. Nobody else complained. Even the smallest of small girl cousins did not complain. They all tried to be as brave as their mothers. But the aunties' heads must be so hard by now, Anna thought. After centuries of pulling and tugging and yanking, their heads must be as hard as tarmac.

Auntie Joly combed Anna Hibiscus's loosened hair. How any knots could have entered it when it had been weaved so

tightly for the whole one week, Anna Hibiscus would never know. But knots were always there. The comb put them there on purpose.

Now it was Anna's turn to have her hair washed. Her mother's fingers were soft and gentle rubbing her sore scalp.

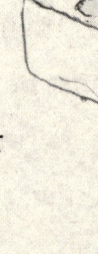

Anna's hair was dried and then oiled and then combed again. Already there were more knots!

This thin comb would tangle anybody's hair, Anna Hibiscus thought crossly.

At last one of the big cousins put Anna's hair into thick easy plaits to keep it neat until tomorrow.

Anna Hibiscus was tired of the pulling and the tugging and the yanking; and tomorrow, she knew, would be worse. Suddenly Anna Hibiscus made a decision.

Tomorrow the Saturday weaving aunties would come. Those Saturday weaving aunties who were not her aunties; who were nobodies' aunties that she knew; who she had to call auntie just to be polite. Tomorrow she would have to sit on the floor between the knees of one of those aunties. And those knees, fat or thin, those knees would grip her head firmly in place. Then the fingers of the Saturday weaving auntie would pull and pull and pull tiny fingerfuls of Anna Hibiscus's hair until Anna was surprised that her hair was not being pulled right out and falling on the ground.

And every Saturday Anna shouted and shouted because she could not help shouting when someone was pulling out fingerfuls of her hair. And everybody would laugh and say, "Anna Hibiscus, you must have a head as soft as a baby!"

Anna was furious just thinking about it.

Next morning, Grandmother and all the aunties and the girl cousins were up early waiting for the Saturday weaving aunties to come and weave their hair. But Anna Hibiscus was up even earlier. Before the first cock crow she peeped out of her bedroom door, looking right, looking left. Then she tiptoed down the corridor.

Oh no! Here was Grandmother! Anna Hibiscus flattened herself against the wall. Grandmother went the other way.

Anna Hibiscus
continued to
tiptoe down
the hall.
Oh no!
Here was
Uncle Tunde!

She peeped down
the stairs. Nobody
there. Nobody except…
Oh no! Anna Hibiscus
shot back into the
corridor. She could
not go down
those stairs
without her
mother seeing her.

Anna Hibiscus tiptoed to another set of stairs that led straight outside. She started to go down… Oh no! Here was Uncle Bizi Sunday! Anna Hibiscus was stuck! The cockerel from next door flew over the wall looking for hens and trouble. Oh no! Now the squawking and the crowing and the shouting would wake everybody up!

Quick, Anna
Hibiscus ran down
the stairs, round
the corner of the
house and jumped
into the back of her
father's car. She ran all
that way and – lucky
for her – nobody saw her.
Not Grandmother, not Mother,
not Uncle Tunde, not Uncle Bizi Sunday,
not the cockerel. Only the hens saw her and
they wouldn't tell.

Now everybody was up. Big cousins rushed
to breakfast untying their plaits. Little cousins
were caught to have their hair loosened.
Aunties chose designs and held little cousins in
place and exchanged news with the Saturday
weaving aunties. Everybody was so loud and
so busy that nobody noticed – Anna Hibiscus
was not there!

It was only just before they left that one of the Saturday weaving aunties asked, "Where dey de small one who like to shout?"

Grandmother, aunties and cousins looked around for Anna Hibiscus.

"It's Anna's turn to oil the little ones' hair!" complained Chocolate. "Anna! Where have you gone?"

Suddenly everybody was asking, "Where is Anna? Where is Anna? Where has Anna Hibiscus gone?"

The big boy cousins were told to look for her high up in the fruit trees.

Chocolate and
Angel were sent to
the girls' bedrooms
to search.

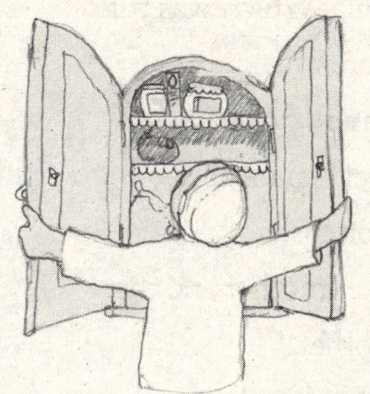

Uncle Tunde
opened cupboards
and took lids off pots.
Anna's mother
texted Anna's father,
who had gone to buy
newspapers. But he
did not know where
Anna was. Anna
Hibiscus was searched
for high and low. Above
and below. Before and
behind. Inside and out.
And she was not found.

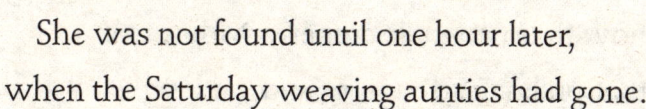

She was not found until one hour later,
when the Saturday weaving aunties had gone.

"Anna Hibiscus, what happened to you?" everybody asked.

"Ah-ah, Anna Hibiscus. We were worrying about you!" said Grandmother.

"I was asleep," said Anna. Which was true. But she did not say *where*.

"Anna Hibiscus, the Saturday weaving aunties, dey have all gone!" said Angel.

"Good!" said Anna Hibiscus.

Anna's grandmother, her mother and the aunties looked at one another.

"But what about your hair?" asked Chocolate, worried.

"I don't care."

The aunties opened their mouths wide-wide.

"Leave her," said Grandmother. "She will learn."

I will, thought Anna happily. I will learn how to do my hair properly without all that pulling and tugging and yanking.

Anna Hibiscus was very proud of herself. She had made a decision and carried it out.

That night, before eating, Anna loosened her thick plaits and put her hair into two neat pompoms. She tied the pompoms with ribbons. It took about two minutes and Anna Hibiscus felt very pretty, and very very happy.

At bedtime, Anna Hibiscus refused to take out the pompoms and put the thick plaits back in.

"Leave her," said Grandmother again.

The next morning, Anna Hibiscus's pompoms were squashed and full of knots.

Anna Hibiscus went to her mother and father's room. She put her father's softening oil on her hair and tried to brush out the knots with her mother's soft brush. The brush stuck fast. Anna had to pull the brush to get it out of her hair. She had to pull it hard. "Ow!" Anna went downstairs with her hair still in squashed pompoms.

Grandfather sent her back upstairs.

"You can't go to church like that," he said.

Anna found a pretty head tie to cover her squashed and knotty pompoms.

"Tomorrow is school," said Cousin Clarity. "You can't go to school with your hair in a head tie. It's not allowed."

On Monday morning, Anna Hibiscus stretched out the squashed and knotty pompoms with her fingers. She could not make them neat. So she just went downstairs. Little cousins looked at her bumpy buldgy hair with big eyes. Big cousins looked with worried eyes. Anna's mother, aunties and uncles and grandmother looked away.

Nobody offered to help Anna Hibiscus, and Anna Hibiscus did not ask for anybody's help. No more pulling and tugging and yanking from them. No, thank you!

At school the other children laughed at Anna

Hibiscus's hair but Anna Hibiscus pretended not to care.

Anna's hair grew worse and worse. Every night more and more knots jumped into her hair, and every morning it was more and more impossible to comb.

On Tuesday morning Anna Hibiscus spent a long time alone with her father's comb. But the knots would not budge. She cried as she tried to comb out the knots and tangles. She cried as she pulled and tugged and yanked her own hair. She cried when the children at school teased her.

On Wednesday morning she took the comb to her mother.

"Oh, Anna!" her mother sighed.

Anna's mother tried to help but Anna's mother's hair was straight; she did not know a lot

about curly hair. The little girl cousins tried to help: they pulled and tugged and yanked. But it was no use. Anna Hibiscus's hair was one big knot.

On Thursday after school the teacher said, "Anna Hibiscus, do not come back until your hair is neat and tidy."

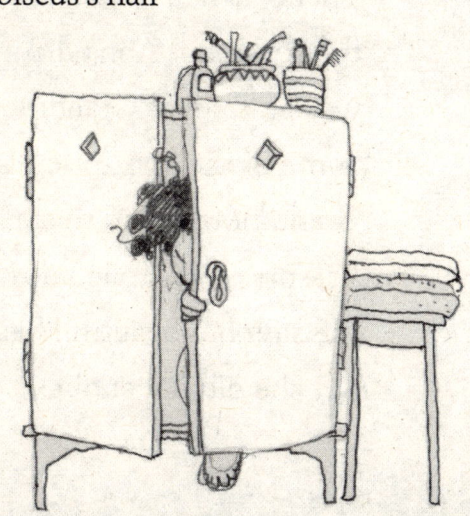

Anna Hibiscus did not tell anybody what the teacher said. But on Friday morning she hid.

After the other cousins had gone to school, Grandmother came to find Anna. Anna's hair was still thicker and curlier than any hair anywhere in the world, but it was no longer shiny and bouncy and beautiful. It was dull and dry and squashed.

"Come with me, Anna Hibiscus," said Grandmother. "Let me help you now."

Grandmother rubbed thick grease in Anna's hair to soften it. She wet it to loosen the knots. She spent a long time softly, softly loosening those knots with her gentle fingers. Then she had to pull and tug and yank with the comb but Anna did not complain. She was grateful to Grandmother for helping her. Some of the knots were so tight that Grandmother had to cut them out with scissors. Tears rolled down Anna's face when she saw her beautiful hair fall to the ground. But she did not shout.

"Anna Hibiscus, your hair! It is short now!" cried the other girl cousins when they saw her.

But Anna Hibiscus did not care. Her problems were over. Grandmother had loosened them and cut them all out.

Anna Hibiscus was happy. Tomorrow the Saturday weaving aunties would come. They would weave her hair into short but beautiful plaits. Plaits that would stay on her head for one whole week, not causing any trouble, not requiring any combing, pulling, tugging or yanking! No more teasing or worrying or hiding. Anna Hibiscus would be able to hold her head high all week!

Saturday came and, for the first time ever, Anna Hibiscus did not shout even one shout.

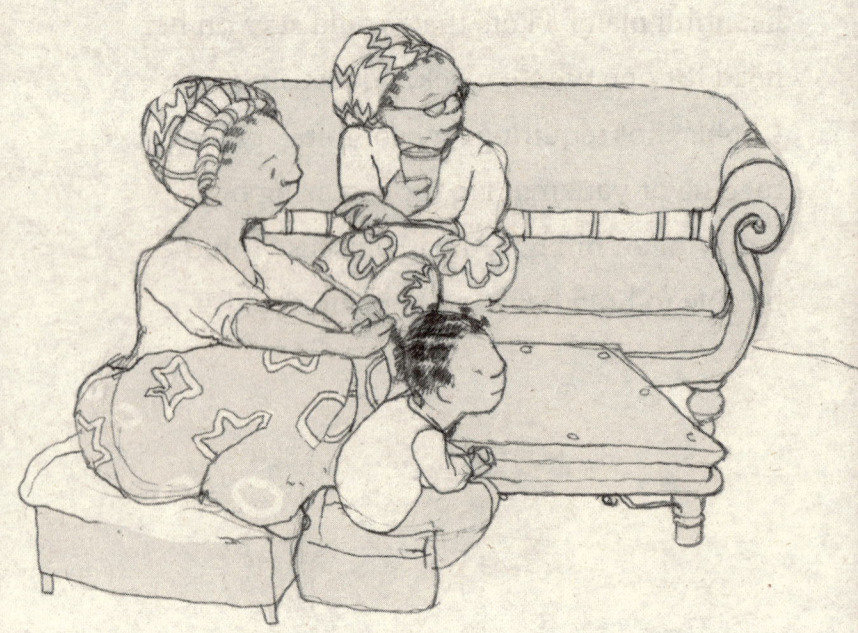

No, while her hair was pulled and tugged and yanked in tiny-tiny fingerfuls, Anna Hibiscus smiled.

Anna Hibiscus and the New Generator

Anna Hibiscus lives in Africa. Amazing Africa. In a country called Nigeria. Na-wa-oh Nigeria! She lives with her whole family in a big white house in a beautiful garden.

Like every other family in Nigeria, the evening is a busy time for Anna's family. Clothes must be washed and rinsed and hung up to dry. Food must be prepared while it is still light.

"Change your clothes!" shouts Auntie Joly at the cousins returning from school.

"Come and pound yam!" calls Anna's mother when she gets home from work.

Anna Hibiscus runs to loose Double from her mother's back. She is too small to pound yam but she is big enough to look after Double, and she is big enough to wash her school clothes ready for the next day.

Food is cooked and eaten and cleared away. It is now dark outside. But in the lit-up house, there is still a lot going on.

The bright and shining house is full of noise. The air conditioners are loud and the television is even louder. Small cousins are crying and whining because they are tired and do not want to go to bed. Double and Trouble whine the loudest of all.

Even outside on the veranda the radio is talking and singing above the voices of the uncles. Only Grandmother and Grandfather are still and quiet, dozing in a corner. Soon Double and Trouble will crawl onto their soft laps and fall asleep.

One night Anna Hibiscus and her cousins were watching television; aunties were sewing on noisy machines; big cousins were homeworking under bright lights; uncles were arguing with the radio.

Suddenly the lights went out! The radio and television were quenched. The air conditioners and sewing machines fell silent.

The electricity was gone!

This is quite normal in Nigeria. If electricity is there, it is there. If it is gone, it is gone. No point asking questions. That is how it is in Nigeria.

Everything is unpredictable. You can count on it.

Now it was **DARK**. Now it was **QUIET**. Anna Hibiscus could see nothing. But she could hear her heart pounding in her chest. She could hear the frogs croak and the mosquitoes whine. She could hear the slap of the lagoon water on the city's dry banks and the roar of the cars in the dark streets. It was dark. It was quiet. It was wonderful!

For a moment, nobody moved, not an inch, not uncles or aunties or cousins. Nobody moved except for Grandmother and Grandfather. They sat bolt upright. Awake! Double and Trouble shuffled on their laps. Then suddenly aunties and uncles and big cousins were calling and searching for matches and candles and torches. Double and Trouble rubbed their eyes.

Anna Hibiscus jumped up and down and yelled, "Hooray! Hooray!"

Little cousins ran shouting. Chocolate and Angel played hide-and-seek in the candlelight and dark. Double and Trouble looked around with big wide eyes at the deep shadows and the dancing yellow candles and the beams of white torchlight. Grandfather made a cool breeze with his fan. It was wonderful.

The big cousins came downstairs. They had to do their homework at the table by the light of the paraffin lamp. Aunties drifted out to talk with uncles on the veranda. There were jokes and laughing. The uncles teased the aunties with songs, and the aunties laughed and danced and softly clapped their hands. The swish-swish of Grandfather's fan joined in.

Then Grandmother told a story. The homework stopped; the jokes and the dancing and the songs stopped. The whole family gathered to listen to Grandmother. Even Double and Trouble sat quietly. One by one the little cousins fell asleep. When Grandmother's stories stopped they would be carried by torchlight to bed. Through the screens of the open bedroom windows the songs of the frogs and the lagoon would last throughout the night.

One evening the aunties and uncles said, "We have an announcement! We have bought a generator. Now when the electricity fails we will still have light!"

The big cousins shouted happily; the aunties exclaimed loudly; Grandmother and Grandfather looked interested. Anna Hibiscus was excited. What did this mean?

Men came with a lorry. A big machine was unloaded and stationed underneath Anna Hibiscus's favourite mango tree. Anna started to look worried.

Two evenings later, the lights went out. The air conditioners and sewing machines and radio and television fell silent. It was dark. It was quiet. It was wonderful. Grandmother and Grandfather sat up. Double and Trouble stirred. The frogs croaked; the lagoon sang. The uncles ran outside to turn on the generator.

A huge engine noise was heard and the lights came back on! The rooms were bright and the television loud again. Cheers and shouts were heard from every corner of the house.

The cousins continued with their homework upstairs. They had not even had time to come down. Triumphant aunties and uncles congratulated each other and went back to their television and radio. Double and Trouble started to cry. Anna Hibiscus and the little cousins looked sadly at one

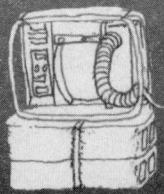

another. There had been no torchlight or candles. There had been no hide-and-seek.

Anna could see Grandmother and Grandfather in the corner. They looked small and old. Grandmother started to say something but nobody heard her. The noise of the generator and the televisions and the radio and the air conditioners and the sewing machines was too loud. Grandmother went back to sleep. The story she would have told was gone.

Grandfather had lifted his fan ready to cool himself, but the air conditioners were already back on. Slowly he lowered it. He looked sadly at Anna Hibiscus and Double and Trouble.

Double and Trouble cried and cried until they were taken upstairs to bed. They were confused; they were upset. Where was the dark, and the quiet, and the wonderful?

Now, every day, the uncles were out with the new generator. Polishing it and oiling it and tightening it up with tools. Double and Trouble and all the cousins, little, medium and big, watched – but they were not allowed to touch.

The new generator was right underneath Anna Hibiscus's favourite mango tree. Now whenever she came out to climb her tree, it was full of big cousins looking down at the generator. It was crowded with uncles and little cousins admiring the generator.

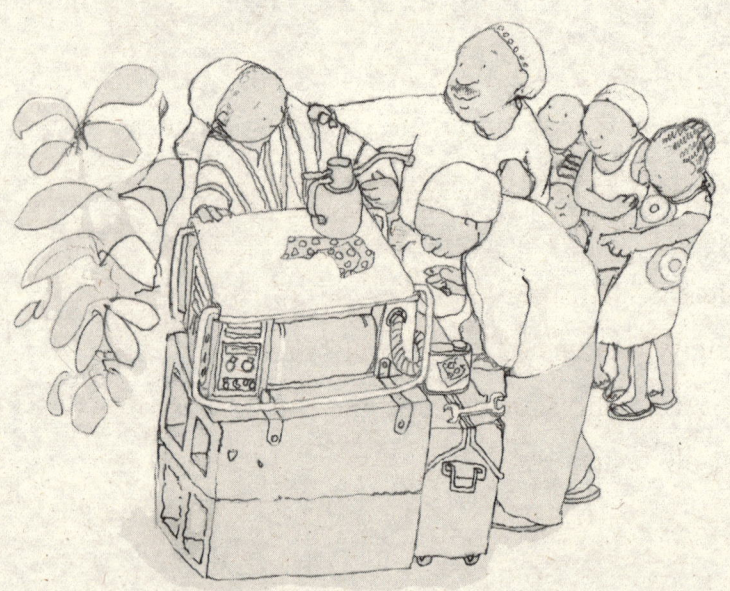

It was busy with friends come to congratulate the family. The ground was littered with tools and oil and rags.

Anna Hibiscus sucked her teeth! This is what you do in Nigeria when you are not at all happy with somebody … or something. Anna Hibiscus sucked her teeth again. What was that machine doing underneath her tree? What was it doing in her compound at all? It had come and swallowed Grandmother's stories, and the songs of the frogs and the lagoon. It had come and blown out the candlelight and the torchlight and the jokes of the aunties and uncles. It had come and stolen the games little cousins played in the dark. It had filled the wide eyes of babies full of tears.

Anna Hibiscus did not like the generator at-all at-all.

There was somebody else who did not like that generator. Somebody else who knew it was in the way. Pronto, the old he-goat with the long, strong horns. Pronto liked to scratch his back on the very same branch the generator stood beneath. Now the generator was blocking the branch.

One day, at last, the uncles and cousins were busy with something else, their friends had gone home and the aunties had returned to their work. Anna Hibiscus climbed her tree alone, in peace. But the generator was still there. Pronto, the old he-goat, was glaring at it.

Suddenly the generator *twanged*! It *wanged* and it *clanged*! Anna Hibiscus clung to her branch and looked down. The generator was alive!

Pronto stared at the big machine. He poked it with one horn. The generator *clanged* and *twanged* again. Now Pronto rammed it with his long, strong horns. If ever a younger he-goat were to walk into the compound, Pronto would deal with him just so.

Anna was frozen on her branch. She did not know what to do!

The old goat was strong, but the generator did not move one inch. Pronto gave up and walked off stiffly. He had not yet succeeded in driving his rival away, but at least he had taught him a lesson.

The generator was silent. A tool came flying out from behind it. The tool was followed first by Trouble and then by Double. Anna Hibiscus's mouth fell open! It had been Double and Trouble *twanging* and *wanging* the generator!

Anna Hibiscus stayed up in the tree for a long time, thinking. She decided to say nothing to anybody. Anna climbed down.

The next time the electricity went off and the aunties went to switch on the generator, it would not start. There was no joking or laughing or dancing that night. The aunties sat sighing at their silent sewing machines. Big cousins stared at each other over their homework. Only the little cousins were happy; only Grandmother and Grandfather were content; only Double and Trouble rubbed their eyes and smiled.

The uncles called a mechanic, but there was nothing he could do. The generator was broken. Kaput. Anna Hibiscus's mother and father, her aunties and uncles and all the big cousins were very sad.

Anna Hibiscus could not stop thinking about Double and Trouble and the generator and Pronto ramming it, and herself up in the tree saying nothing and still saying nothing now! Anna Hibiscus could not stop thinking, but she did not know what to do.

Grandmother and Grandfather noticed. They noticed that when the lights went out, Anna Hibiscus no longer shouted "Hooray!" She no longer laughed and ran and played hide-and-seek.

One day when the house was quiet and empty they called her.

"What is the matter, Anna Hibiscus?" Grandfather asked.

"Nothing, Grandfather," replied Anna.

"Are you missing the generator?" Grandmother asked gently.

Anna burst into tears.

Grandmother and Grandfather looked at each other. Anna Hibiscus told them the whole story. She told them how the generator had come alive and how Pronto had rammed it, and how a tool had come flying out from behind it followed by Double and Trouble.

Grandmother and Grandfather laughed and laughed. They could not stop. Double and Trouble crawled over to join in the fun. They did not know why Grandmother and Grandfather were laughing, but they wanted to laugh too.

"Hooray!" shouted Double happily.

Now Anna started to laugh. She could not help herself. Grandmother and Grandfather, Anna Hibiscus, and Double and Trouble laughed and laughed.

That night, when the whole family was gathered to eat, Grandfather made an announcement.

"Generators," said Grandfather, "are very untraditional. They are guzzlers of money. They are destroyers of the peace. God has ordained some nights for modern busy noisiness, and others for more traditional pursuits. God gives us electricity some nights and takes it away other nights. This is a balance between modern and traditional. Our family will spend no more money on disturbing this balance. No more generators in this compound!"

Anna Hibiscus breathed a sigh of relief. Now she need not say anything about Double and Trouble and Pronto and the generator to anybody else. They had probably been acting under Grandfather's orders. Or God's.

That night, in the dark and quiet,
Grandmother's stories were about
an old he-goat, troublesome but wise!

The Other Side of the City

Anna Hibiscus lives with her mother and her father; her grandmother and her grandfather; her aunties and their husbands; her uncles and their wives; all her many, many cousins; and her two baby brothers. They all live together in a big white house in a large quiet compound in the huge busy city of Lagos in the wonderful country of Nigeria on the amazing continent of Africa.

The city that Anna Hibiscus lives in is full of roads and lagoons, full of cars and boats, full of people. Poor people and rich people, all rush and hurry. Anna's compound is quiet – much quieter than the busy-busy city outside the gate with its millions of people and thousands of roads and hundreds of lagoons.

Anna Hibiscus often looks through the gate to the lagoon on the other side of the road. It is crowded with boats coming and going from the other side of the city.

"Come and play, Anna Hibiscus," said Cousin Sweetheart one day.

"Why are you always looking outside?" asked Cousin Joy.

Anna wanted to go on the ferry across the lagoon. Anna wanted to see the other side of the city. That was why she was always looking and looking.

"What can there be to see?" asked Cousin Wonderful. "It can only be more houses like this. More people like us."

But still Anna wanted to go. Still Anna had to see.

Uncle Bizi Sunday often went on one of those lagoon ferry boats. Uncle Bizi Sunday had people he went to see on the other side of the city. Anna Hibiscus decided to ask him, again, to take her.

"Stop troubling me!" said Uncle Bizi Sunday.

Auntie Joly also went to the other side of the city. She took clothes sometimes to a home for motherless babies there. Anna decided to ask her.

"Anna Hibiscus," Auntie Joly sighed, "why do you want to go to the other side of the city? The people there are poor. It is not a good place. The other side of the city has nothing to do with you."

So Anna Hibiscus asked Uncle Tunde and her other uncles.

She asked Auntie Grace and her other aunties.

They all said the same thing. "It is a poor place. It is not a good place. Why does it concern you?"

Anna asked Grandmother and Grandfather, "Is it bad to be poor? Is it wrong?"

"No," said Grandmother. "It is not bad. It is not wrong. But it is not easy to be very poor."

"It is not easy to look at poverty either," Anna's mother added.

"It is not enjoyable to be very poor and it is not enjoyable to see, Anna Hibiscus," said her father. "The other side of the city is not for you."

But still Anna Hibiscus wanted to go.

"Let her go," said Grandfather. "Let her see; let her know."

Anna Hibiscus jumped up and down! Hooray! Hooray! She was going on a ferry. She was going to cross the lagoon. She was going to see the other side of the city!

"Thank you, Grandfather! Thank you!" she shouted, and ran to tell Sweetheart and Joy and Wonderful and all the other cousins.

"Let her see and know just how lucky she is," said Grandfather, sighing.

Anna Hibiscus got ready. She oiled her neatly plaited hair. She chose her best pink Sunday dress, her favourite hair ribbons and her new Sunday shoes.

"Remove the shoes," said Auntie Joly. "Do you want to spoil them in the boat?"

Anna Hibiscus put her shoes back in the cupboard. She put on her old pink flip-flops. All flip-flops Anna's size were pink. Other sizes were other colours.

Auntie Joly and Uncle Bizi Sunday were going to take Anna on the ferry. Auntie Joly wore one of her old dresses; Uncle Bizi Sunday wore his working clothes. Only Anna Hibiscus looked pretty and smart. Grandmother sighed when she saw her. But she didn't say why.

Down by the lagoon there were many, many people all pushing and squeezing and rushing to get on and off the ferry. Anna Hibiscus held tight to Uncle Bizi Sunday's hand. A man with strong legs was keeping the ferry in place. He had one foot on the jetty and one foot in the ferry. Auntie Joly jumped onto the ferry. Uncle Bizi Sunday jumped onto the ferry. Anna Hibiscus had to jump too. She had to jump if she wanted to go to the other side of the city.

Uncle Bizi Sunday held out his arms to Anna Hibiscus. As Anna jumped, a big woman jumped too, bumping Anna and rocking the ferry. Anna almost fell into the lagoon, but Uncle Bizi Sunday caught her arm quick-quick and pulled her into the boat. One of Anna Hibiscus's pink flip-flops fell into the lagoon. It floated away with the rest of the rubbish under the boat and was gone.

"Do you want to kill my brother's child?" Auntie Joly shouted. "Wha' kind of woman are you? Ca' you not see a child when she is jumping in front of you?"

Quickly the big woman said, "Sorry, ma. Sorry." She looked at Anna Hibiscus. "Don' cry. Don' cry," she said.

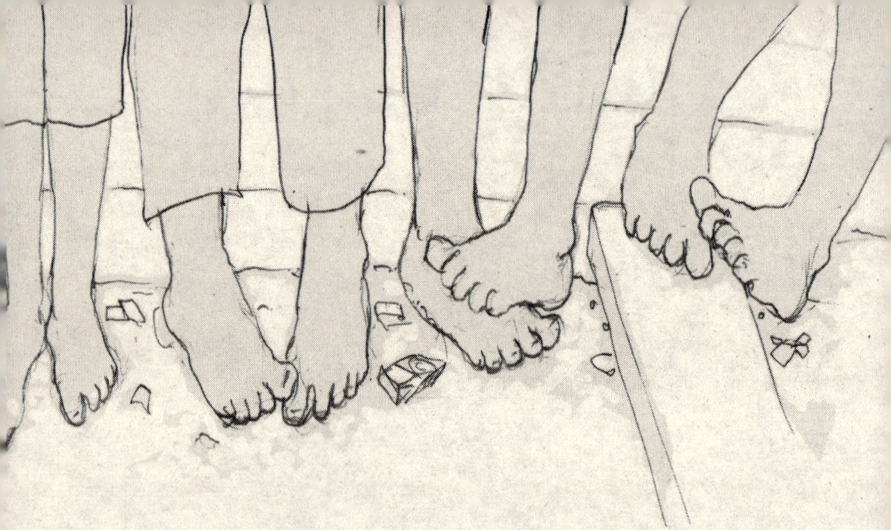

Anna Hibiscus could not stop crying. She had almost fallen into the lagoon. Her arm was hurting where Uncle Bizi Sunday had pulled her into the boat. Her dress was dirty and one of her flip-flops was lost for ever.

"Don' cry!" said Uncle Bizi Sunday. "You are not the only one without shoes."

Anna Hibiscus looked. Most of the people on the ferry had no shoes. Their bare feet

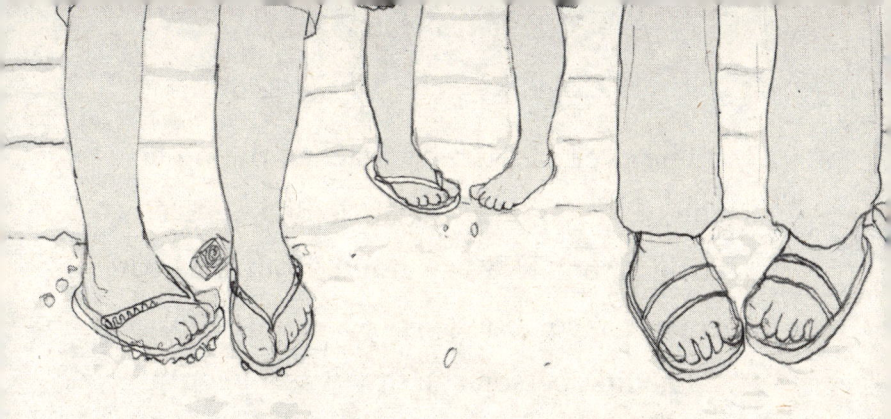

rested in the rubbish and the dirty water
in the bottom of the boat. Just like Anna's
one bare foot.

Anna stopped crying. She kept on her
other flip-flop. What else could she do? Anna
Hibiscus worried. Would people on the other
side of the city notice her beautiful dress
and her pretty ribbons and her shiny hair,
or would they only notice her one shoe?

The overloaded ferry reached the other side of the lagoon and Uncle Bizi Sunday carried Anna Hibiscus down from the boat. Anna looked about.

The first person she saw was a beggar girl holding her hands out for coins. Her hair was ragged and matted into dusty dirty clumps. She had no legs.

The beggar girl looked at Anna Hibiscus and called out, "Fine girl, help me. Fine girl, help your sister!"

Anna Hibiscus did not know what to do. She did not want to look at the beggar girl with no legs. She had no money to help this new "sister" who was like no other girl she had seen before, rich or poor. So Anna hid behind Auntie Joly until they had moved away.

Now Anna Hibiscus could look again. All around were many, many people wearing torn and faded clothes. The roads were narrow and the gutters stank like toilets. There were many, many houses all squeezed together. One-room houses made of old rotting wood and rusty corrugated iron patched with cardboard boxes. Among them were big piles of rotting rubbish. The sound of babies crying and people shouting filled the air.

Anna Hibiscus had never seen anything like this before. She wanted to close her eyes and close her nose and close her ears and make it all go away, but her eyes and nose and ears stayed open and wide. She held tight to Auntie Joly's hand.

Auntie Joly and Uncle Bizi Sunday stopped outside a one-room house made of corrugated iron full of rusty holes. A weak voice called for them to enter. It was hot inside. The sun beat down on the iron walls and roof, heating the room like an oven. It was too hot for Anna Hibiscus.

"Anna Hibiscus, go and wait for us outside," Auntie Joly said after she had greeted the sick old woman lying on a mat.

Outside, it was not so hot. The sun still beat down but there was air. Close to Anna Hibiscus was a pile of rubbish. A big pile of rubbish. There were children climbing all over it.

Anna went closer. The children were naked or clothed in rags. They were picking things out of the rubbish. They were *eating* the rubbish!

Anna Hibiscus could not blink or even think. Suddenly she no longer knew why she was wearing her best pink Sunday dress and her favourite ribbons. She hoped none of the children would notice, or they would know she did not have to eat rubbish. They would know she had pretty dresses while they ate rubbish.

Anna Hibiscus saw one girl dressed only in ragged underpants pick a flip-flop out of the rubbish. It was pink. The same as Anna's. The girl tried it on. It fitted. She was the same size as Anna Hibiscus!

The girl saw Anna Hibiscus watching her. They looked at each other and the girl frowned. Anna Hibiscus was wearing her best pink dress. She had pretty ribbons in her hair. The girl was wearing ragged grey underpants. Her hair was all cut off. But they were both wearing only one pink flip-flop. Anna Hibiscus smiled at the girl. The girl gave Anna Hibiscus a crooked smile back.

Slowly Anna Hibiscus took off her one pink flip-flop. She held it out to the girl.

The girl shook her head and frowned.
So Anna Hibiscus put her flip-flop on the pile
of rubbish and turned her back on it. Quickly,
before anyone else could, the other girl
picked up the pink flip-flop and put it on.

Anna Hibiscus looked round and saw the
girl skipping away down the street in her
matching pink flip-flops. Anna gazed at the
other naked ragged children. She thought of
her many dresses hanging in the cupboard
in her room. Then Anna Hibiscus took off her
dress. She took it off right there in the street
and threw it onto the
rubbish heap.

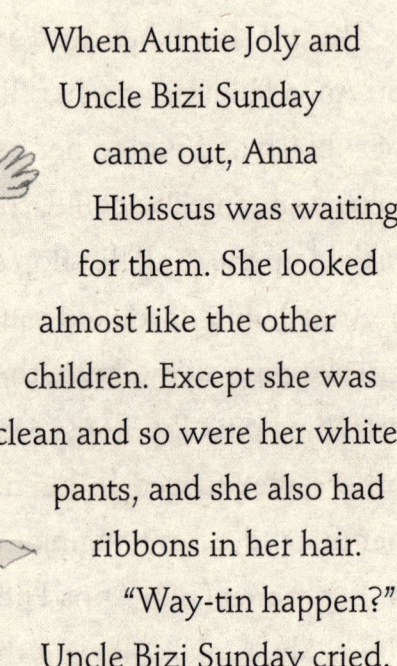

When Auntie Joly and Uncle Bizi Sunday came out, Anna Hibiscus was waiting for them. She looked almost like the other children. Except she was clean and so were her white pants, and she also had ribbons in her hair.

"Way-tin happen?" Uncle Bizi Sunday cried.

"Anna Hibiscus!" shouted Auntie Joly. "What kind of nonsense is this?"

Anna Hibiscus did not answer. She was watching a small girl dancing down the road in a pink Sunday dress. She looked at Auntie Joly and Uncle Bizi Sunday and smiled her biggest smile.

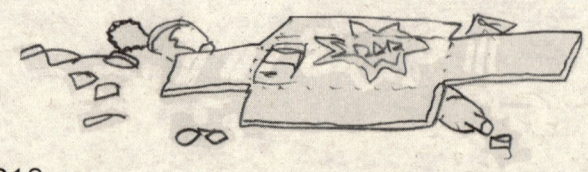

Auntie Joly gasped and closed her eyes. Uncle Bizi Sunday shook his head. "Anna Hibiscus!" he said.

"Grandmother will deal with you at home, Anna Hibiscus," Auntie Joly said, and she led her back to the ferry.

The beggar girl was still there by the jetty. She saw Anna Hibiscus. Anna did not look so fine now. But she was feeling better than before. She took her favourite ribbons from her hair and tied them softly, softly in the matted hair of the beggar girl with no legs.

The beggar girl looked at Anna Hibiscus with wide eyes. "God bless you!" she whispered.

And that is exactly what Grandmother said after Anna Hibiscus explained to the gathered family why she had come home in only her underpants.

"Hooray!" said Double.

"Hooray for Anna 'biscus!" said Trouble.

Atinuke was born in Nigeria and spent her childhood in both Africa and the UK. She is the author of the bestselling Anna Hibiscus and No. 1 Car Spotter series set in contemporary Nigeria, as well as award winning non-fiction books *Africa, Amazing Africa: Country by Country* and *Brilliant Black British History*. Atinuke is also an oral storyteller of tales from the African continent and diaspora. She currently lives on a mountain overlooking the sea in West Wales. Visit her website at atinuke.co.uk

Lauren Tobia lives in Bristol. She shares her little house with her husband and their grumpy cat called Dora. When Lauren is not drawing, she can be found drinking tea on her allotment.